Withdrawn

Snug
in Mama's
Arms

by *Angela Shelf Medearis* • illustrated by *John Sandford*

To my mother, Angeline Shelf; my sisters, Marcia Shelf Orlandi and Sandra Fergins; and my daughter, Deanna Medearis—great mothers all. And to all the women who mother me, with love and thanks.

—Angela Shelf Medearis

For Sugar Grandma Clara Tate with love

—JS

The artist wishes to thank D'Kyah and Ericka English for their generous help in the making of this book.

 Children's Publishing

Text © 2004 Angela Shelf Medearis
Illustrations © 2004 McGraw-Hill Children's Publishing

This edition published in the United States of America in 2004 by
Gingham Dog Press
an imprint of McGraw-Hill Children's Publishing,
a Division of The McGraw-Hill Companies
8787 Orion Place
Columbus, Ohio 43240-4027

www.MHkids.com

Library of Congress Cataloging-in-Publication Data is on file with the publisher.

Printed in The United States of America.

1-57768-430-3

1 2 3 4 5 6 7 8 9 10 PHXBK 09 08 07 06 05 04

Aligned to State & National Standards!
Visit MHkids.com

Students must meet state standards to be adequately prepared for proficiency testing.
To learn more about how McGraw-Hill Children's Publishing aligns its books to state standards, visit www.MHkids.com.

◀Align
to Achieve
The Academic Standards e-Library

The McGraw-Hill Companies

I'll read you one more story,
and then it's time for bed.

You're yawning and you're nodding,
my little sleepyhead.

Bring Kangaroo and Mr. Bear
to rock with us a while.

You are snug in Mama's arms,
where dreams stretch on for miles.

All your toys are sleepy too.
They're tucked in for the night.

You've given them each one last hug.
Now let's turn out the light.

The moon has on its nightcap,
and a soft wind gently snores.

All the animals are tucked away in nature's bed outdoors.

In pastures, barns, and meadows,

horses, cows, and sheep,

ducklings, pups, and piglets, too,

have drifted off to sleep.

Each mother bird and baby bird

have nestled in the trees,

while daddy fish and baby fish

rock gently in the seas.

The moon has slipped behind the clouds.
A soft rain's gently falling.

But you are snug in Mama's arms,
and peaceful dreams are calling.

In igloos and on sampans,

in hogans and on farms,

children all around the world
are snug in mamas' arms.

Someone's sleeping soundly
with dreaming eyes closed tight,
safe and snug in Mama's arms.
Sleep well, my love. Good night.